P9-CFG-434

Somewhere in the Italian hills, a homing Pigeon is released. She soars Quickly and follows an old road, which (of course) leads to Rome.

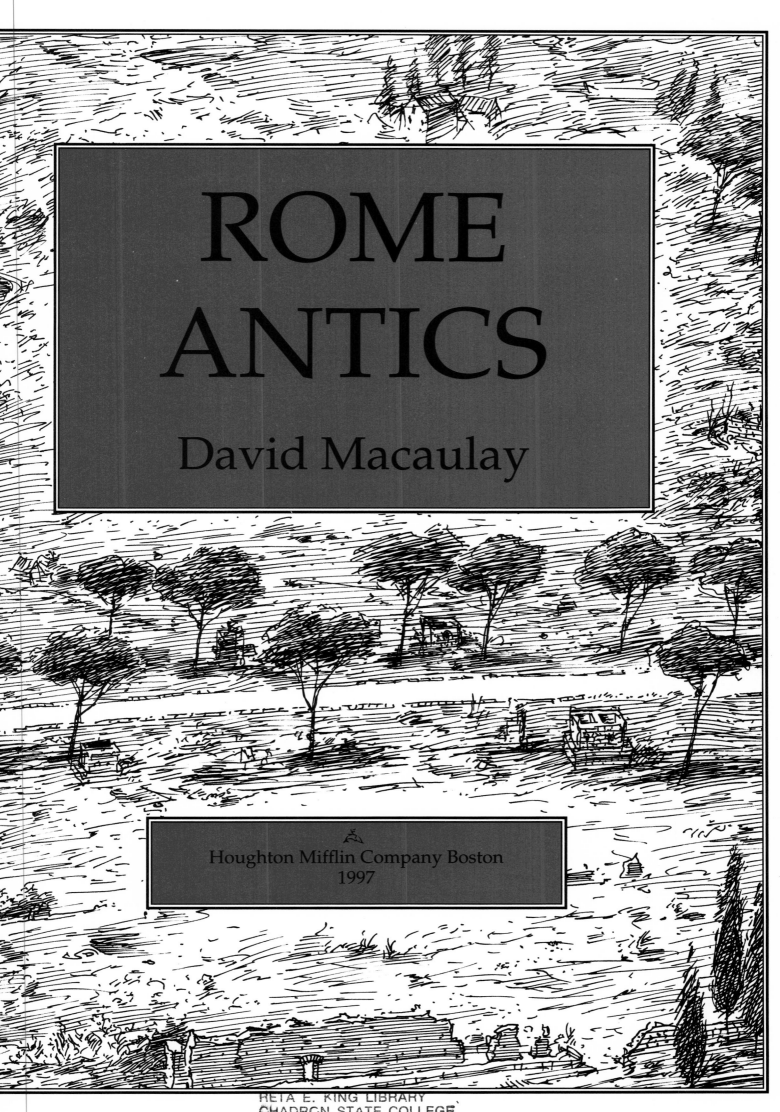

ROME ANTICS

David Macaulay

Houghton Mifflin Company Boston
1997

For Ruthie

Appian Way

After a couple of hours, the sight of ancient tombs and the sound of distant car horns tell her she is getting close.

Aurelian Wall

Finally, she sees the high brick wall that once surrounded the city, but now just interrupts it.

Pyramid of Caius Cestius   Porta Ostiense

As she approaches an abandoned gatehouse,
a most unprofessional thought enters her head.

Arch of Constantine   Colosseum

Instead of traveling directly to her destination, which is standard pigeon procedure, she decides to take the scenic route.

Colosseum

In no time she is circling the most famous amphitheater in the world, still standing room only after all these centuries.

The Forum   Palatine Hill

Across the road, pieces of building — some marble, some brick —
are sprouting up among the wildflowers and equally wild cats.

Santa Maria in Cosmedin   Temple of Hercules

Chiming midday bells draw her over the hill, where streams of
cars roar up and down both sides of the river.

Tiber River   Ponte Fabricio

To avoid the traffic, she dives below the high embankments
and follows her reflection upstream.

Palazzo Spada

Back over dry land, she meets an unusual bird who says nothing.

Sun-warmed terra-cotta rooftops are tempting
places to land. But a pigeon must be careful.

Palazzo Farnese

Trees and flowers in a private garden remind her of the country.

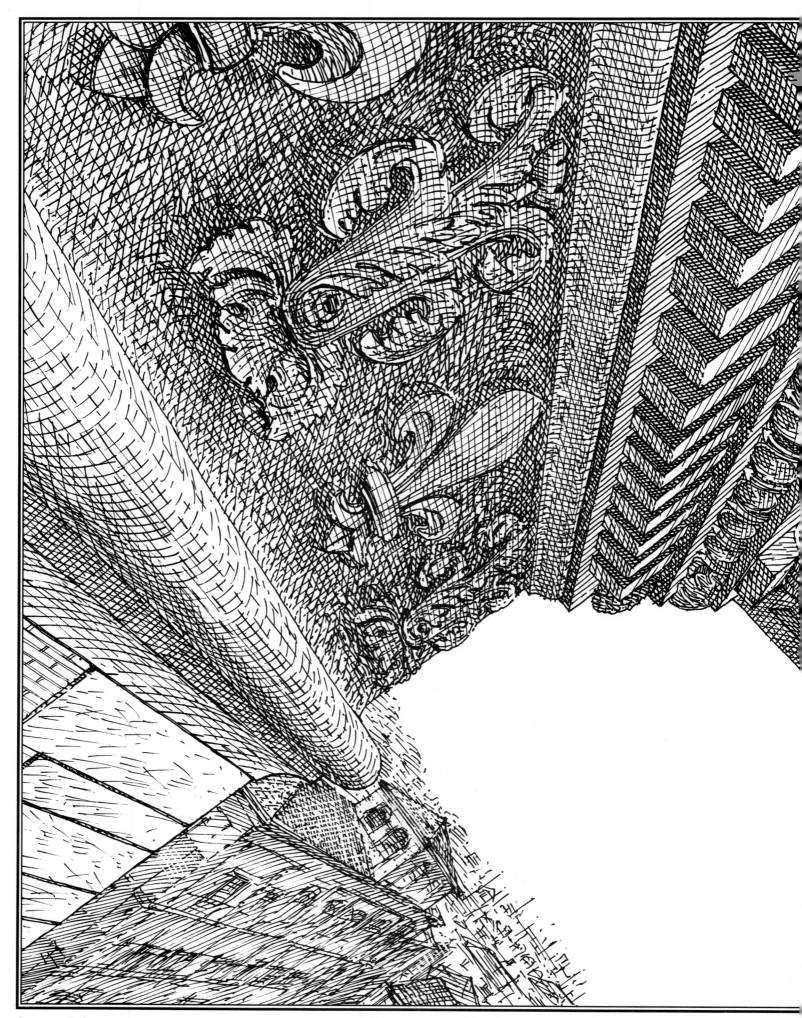

Cornice, Palazzo Farnese

Distracted and a little homesick, she narrowly
avoids a disastrous encounter.

Campo dei Fiori

But she is soon comforted by the sight and smell of food in a market square.

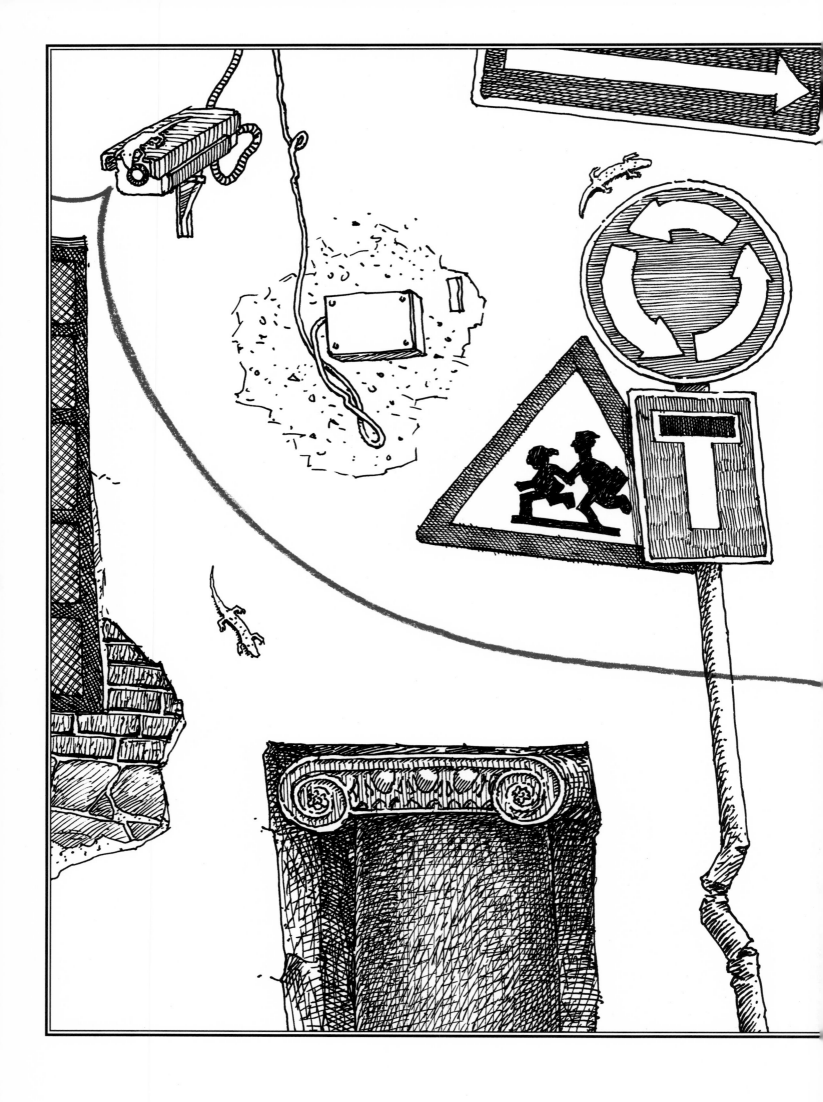

Feeling a little hungry, she follows her beak down narrow streets in search of crumbs.

An attempt to snack between the cobblestones is rudely interrupted
by a careless scooter, driving her back to the safety of the sky.

Still hungry, she flies on, but now her wings are getting tired.

Once again she tries to land. Once again she is denied.

Santa Maria della Pace

A sudden collision sends her reeling.

Perhaps the scenic route was not such a good idea.

Torre Millina   Sant'Agnese in Agone

Somewhat discombobulated, she struggles
to regain her composure and her bearings.

Sant'Agnese in Agone   Piazza Navona

At last she spies a row of restaurants and approaches without reservation.

Sant'Agnese in Agone   Piazza Navona

She finds a soft warm place to rest and is about to
close her eyes when a cell phone rudely bleeps.

Sant'Ivo alla Sapienza

Startled back into the sky, she flies towards
a large but unfortunately inedible confection.

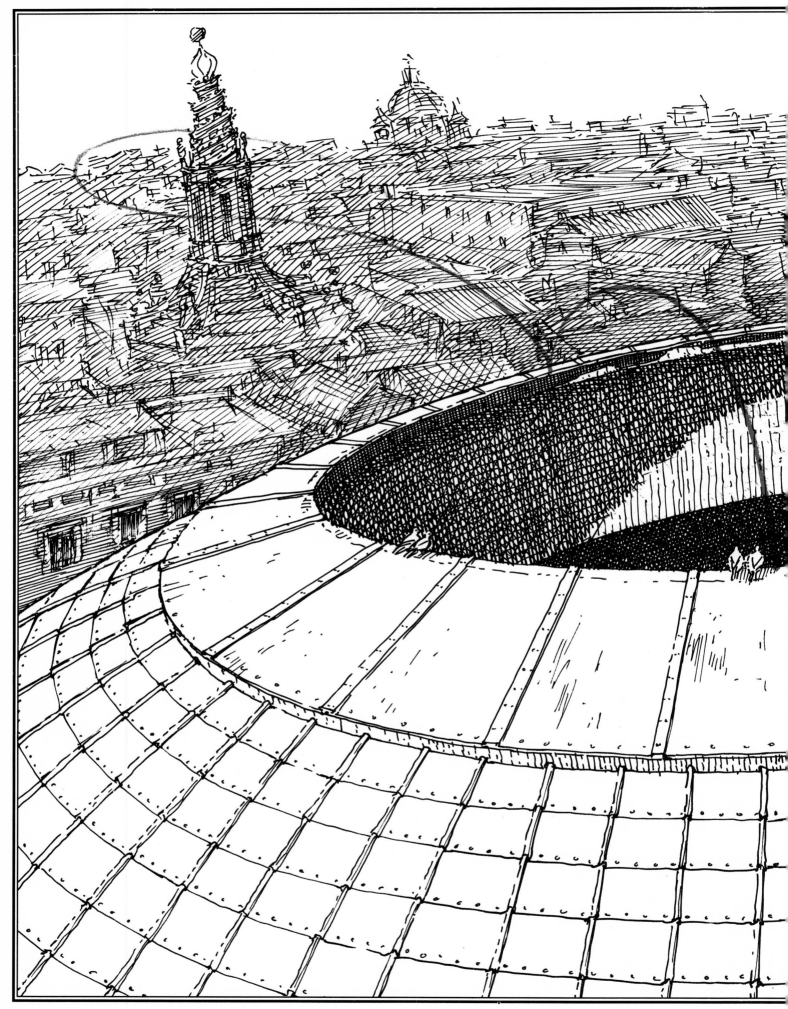

Pantheon

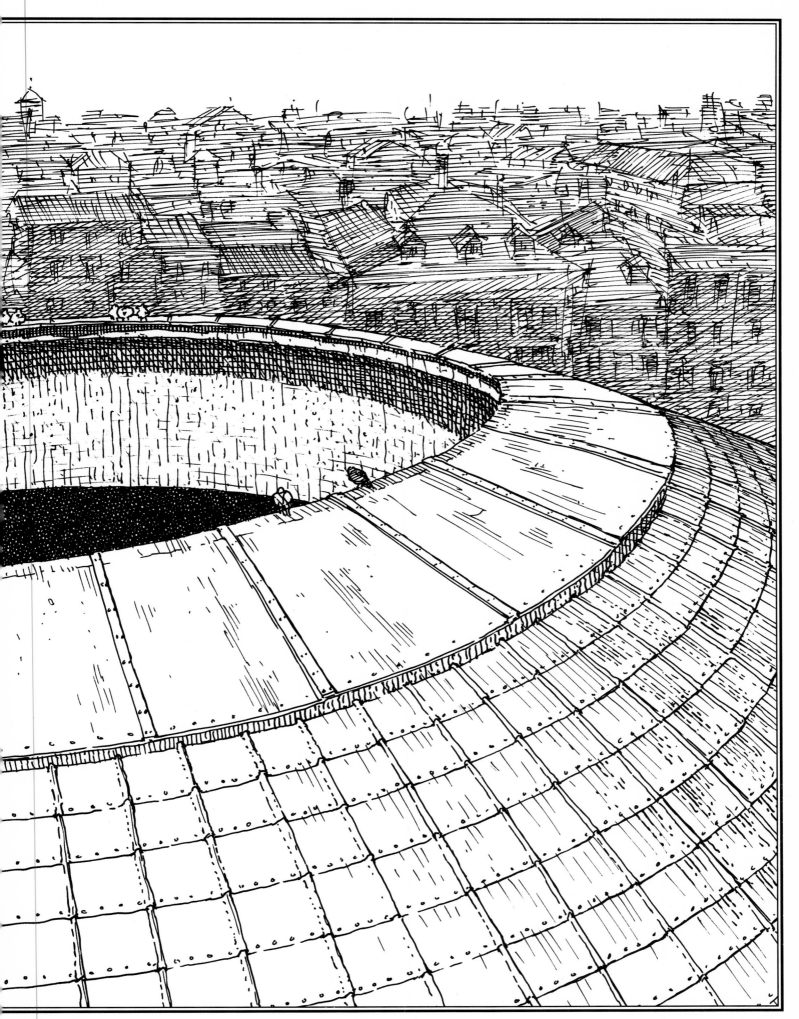

Barely stopping to catch her breath, she disappears into a gaping hole.

Pantheon

Through the darkness she descends towards an open door.

Pantheon

Blinding sunlight and an imposing granite column temporarily impede her progress.

Pantheon

Slightly bruised, she considers entering the daily sleeping contest held on the entablature. But there is work to be done.

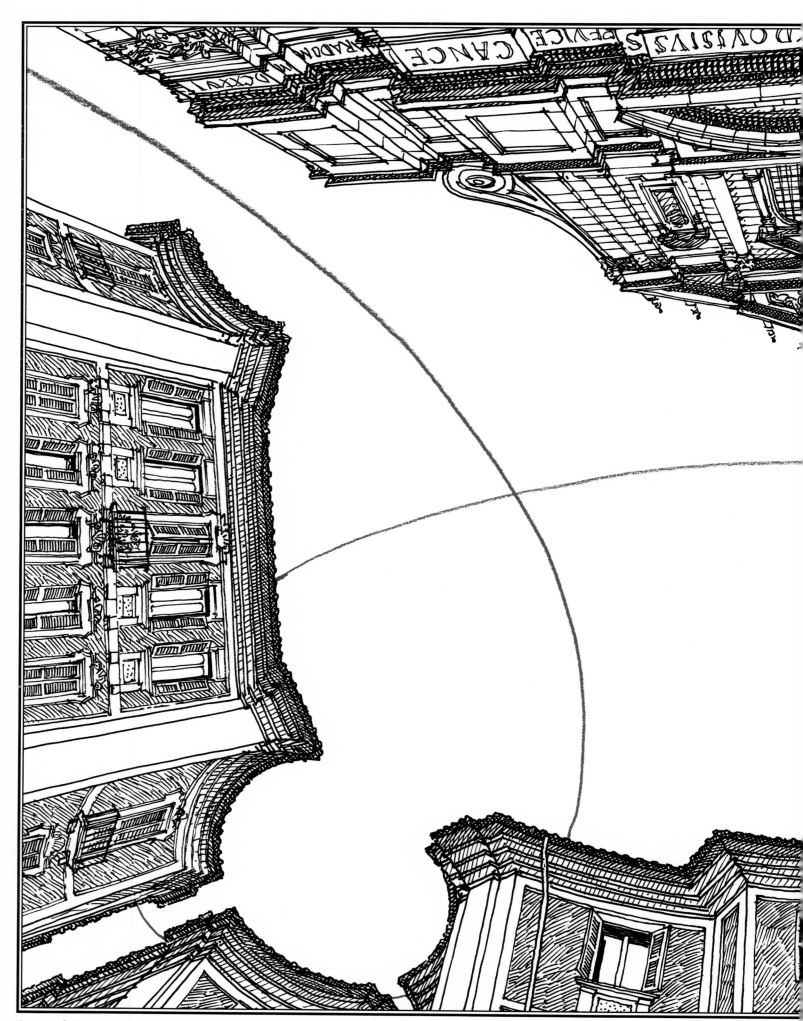

Piazza di Sant'Ignazio

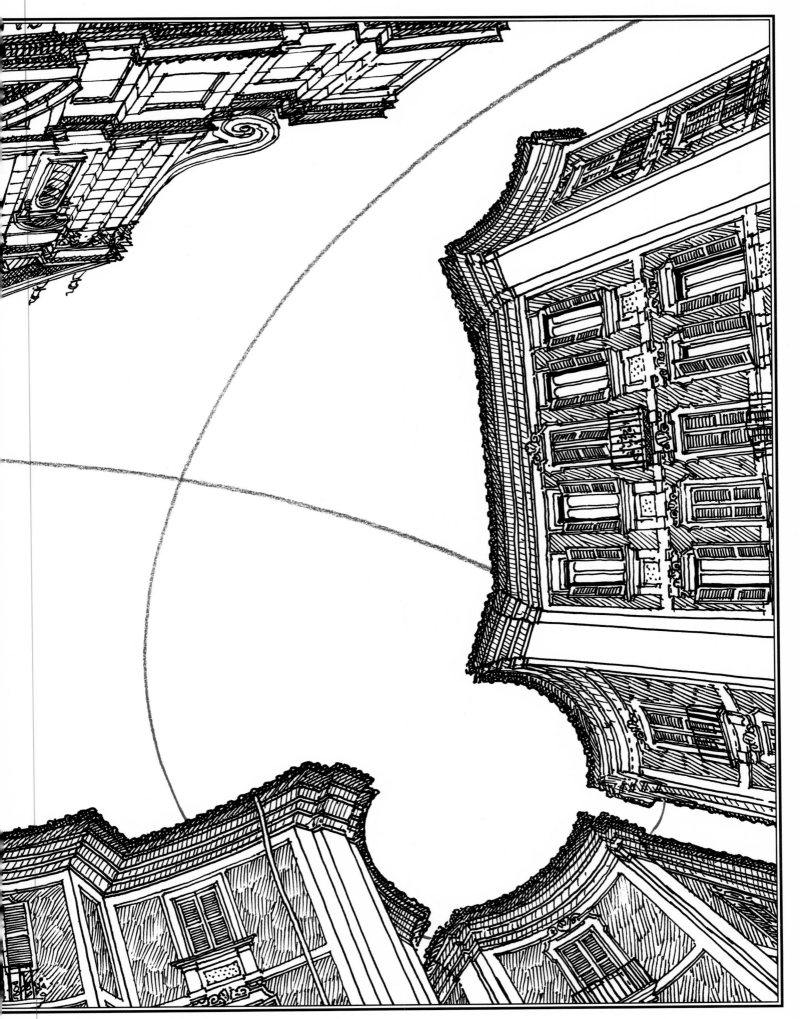

She firmly resolves to stay on course, at least until she reaches this piazza.

The Gesù

After which a marble scroll inspires more athletic behavior.

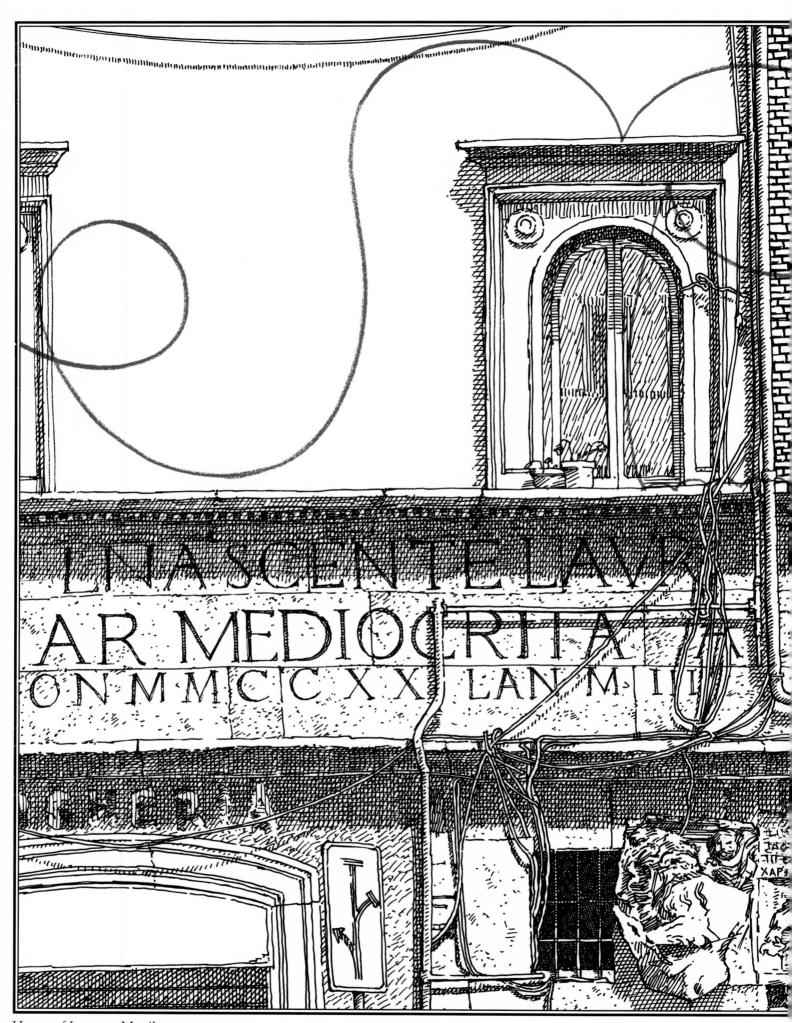

House of Lorenzo Manilo

Then a wall where centuries meet encourages further investigation.

Suddenly a shaking mop brings her to her senses.

Two squawking birds remind her to avoid the dog (who is no threat).

But they forget to mention the cat (who is).
Straight up and in, she arrives at last.

The man removes a strip of paper from her leg.
They are both breathing hard as he reads the message.

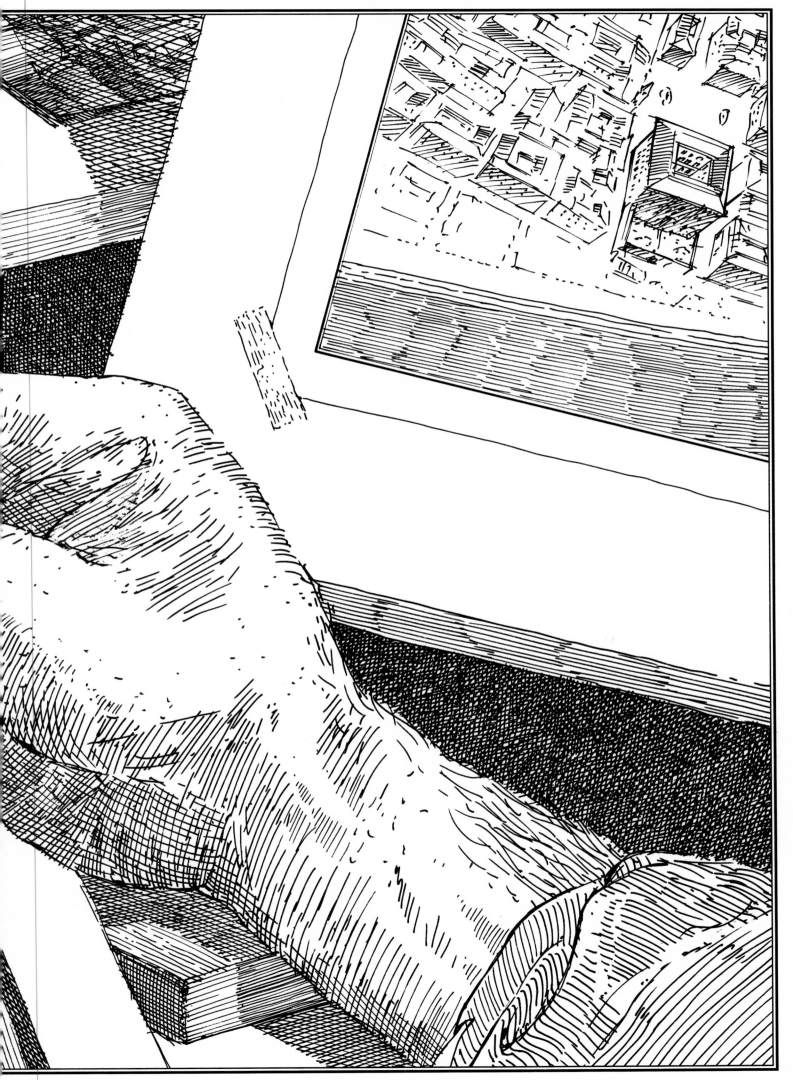

Corso Vittorio Emanuele II

Via Arenula

TIBER RIVER

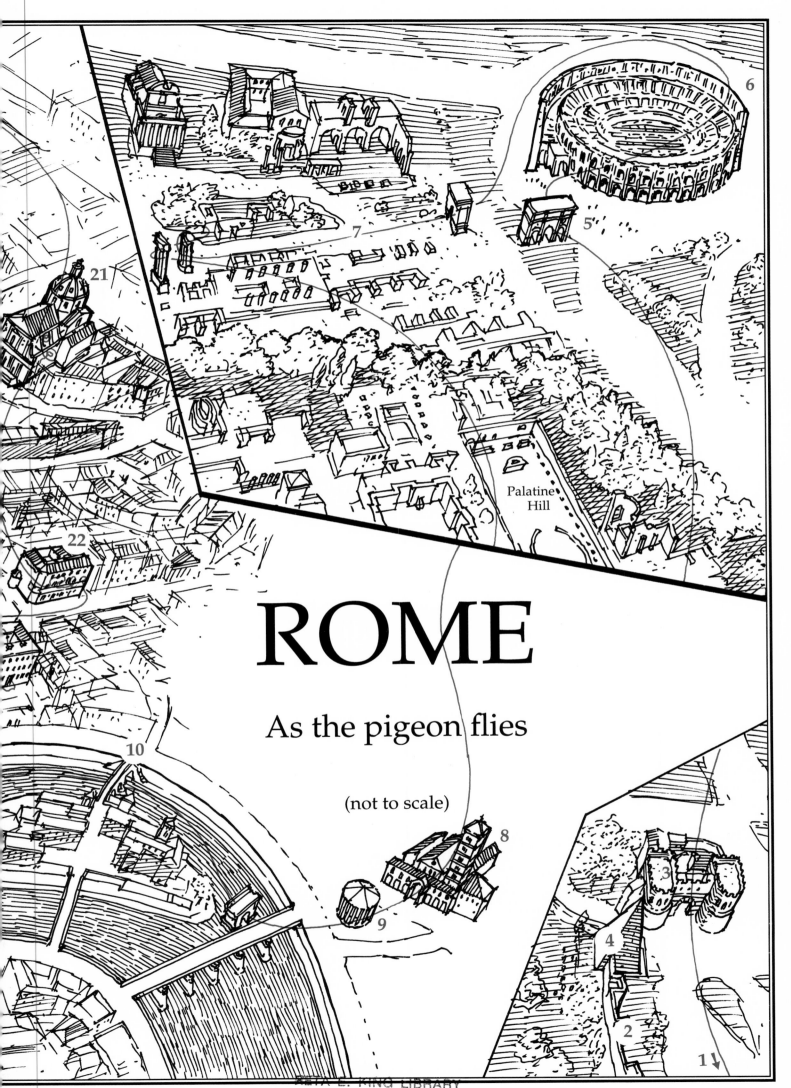

ROME

As the pigeon flies

(not to scale)

Palatine
Hill

1. Appian Way

Roman engineers were both practical and thorough, which is why the roads they built were straight and durable. The Appian Way is one such road. It was begun in 312 B.C. to connect Rome and Capua, and was eventually extended to the port city of Brindisi, covering a distance of more than three hundred miles. Lining the Appian Way are numerous ruins, including many tombs. The Romans buried their dead outside the city walls. This wasn't so much a matter of neatness as it was religious custom and law.

2. Aurelian Wall

In the fourth century B.C. Rome was enclosed for the first time by a stone wall. Over the centuries the city grew, and by A.D. 270 a much longer wall was needed. Begun by the Emperor Aurelius, it was to be eleven miles long and approximately thirty feet high. Thirty years later, Emperor Maxentius added another thirty feet to the wall's height, which is what we see today. By the nineteenth century, the wall once built to enclose the city had gradually become enclosed by it.

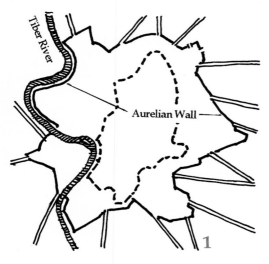

3. Porta Ostiense

In addition to almost four hundred watchtowers, eighteen gatehouses were built into the eleven-mile-long wall to control all comings and goings. Maxentius added the stonework to a number of the gatehouses, including the Porta Ostiense, to make them look a little more impressive. It worked.

4. Pyramid of Caius Cestius

One of the best-preserved and most unusual tombs was built in 12 B.C. by Caius Cestius, a wealthy and important Roman magistrate. Importance, however, does not always guarantee permanence. When the Aurelian Wall went up two centuries later, the Egyptian-style tomb was simply incorporated into it, reducing the cost of labor and materials.

5. Arch of Constantine

This triumphal arch was built in A.D. 315 to honor the Emperor Constantine. Some of the sculpture is from the time of Constantine, while other pieces were already one or two centuries old, having been made to celebrate the exploits of his predecessors Trajan and Marcus Aurelius. Not only is this arch an impressive gateway, it is also another example of Roman practicality—recycling in the service of ego.

6. Colosseum

The Colosseum hasn't stopped working since it was built nineteen hundred years ago. It is an amphitheatre in which approximately fifty thousand people at a time could enjoy a variety of entertainment, all of which had to do with one kind of creature killing another. These bloody shows ran for four hundred years, until they were finally banned. A thousand years ago all the vaulted passages surrounding the arena were being used as houses, storerooms, workshops, and even a church. In the thirteenth century the structure was converted into a fortress, and starting in the fifteenth century it was quarried extensively for its high-quality Travertine building stone.

7. The Forum

When Rome was the center of the empire, the Forum was the administrative, judicial, and commercial center of Rome. In 46 B.C. Julius Caesar began building the Forum we see today. Over the next four hundred years, each emperor added new buildings. Today it is filled with the remains of basilicas, temples, and roads, not to mention two more triumphal arches and an undetermined number of cats.

8. Santa Maria in Cosmedin

Although the earliest parts of the church of Santa Maria in Cosmedin were built in the sixth century, the high brick bell tower wasn't added until the twelfth. This is when a lot of other churches around the city were acquiring their own bell towers. The bells of Rome still announce important events and help keep track of the time.

9. Temple of Hercules

This temple was built in the second century B.C. to honor Hercules Olivarius, the protector of the oil merchants' guild of the port. This explains its location right by the Tiber River, which at that time would have been lined with docks. It is still in good condition because in the Middle Ages it was reconsecrated as a Christian church and has therefore been well cared for. In fact, it is now covered in scaffolding and undergoing a major restoration. The words most feared by visitors to Rome are *Chiuso per Restauro.* They mean "Closed for Restoration" and invariably appear on the very building you came specially to see. But look on the bright side. Without this kind of attention, Rome wouldn't have its extraordinary collection of buildings spanning two thousand years.

10. Ponte Fabricio

Rome grew up along both sides of the Tiber, which meant that either ferry boats or bridges were required from the earliest days. The Ponte Fabricio, built in 62 B.C., is the oldest bridge in the city and is still in use. It was built by the road commissioner Lucius Fabricius, who was apparently very proud of this structure. His name appears on it in four places.

11. Palazzo Spada

Palazzo Spada was built around 1540. The elaborate façade is encrusted with symbols of ancient Roman glory, including statues of several emperors. All the ornamentation is made of a heavy plaster called stucco. This is the same material that covers most of the buildings in Rome, but rarely with this degree of elaborateness or skill.

12. Palazzo Farnese

Just up the street from Palazzo Spada is the largest palazzo in Rome. The Palazzo Farnese was begun in 1534 and was not finished for almost sixty years. As in most palazzi, the rooms of the Farnese surround an open courtyard, which provides extra light, better ventilation, and private outdoor space. Both the Farnese and the Spada palaces are among the few that have separate large gardens in addition to courtyards. The building is mostly brick and cement. Stone, said to be from the Colosseum, was used to highlight the corners and surround windows and doors. The impressive cornice that formally defines the top of the building was designed by Michelangelo, who is also known for other things.

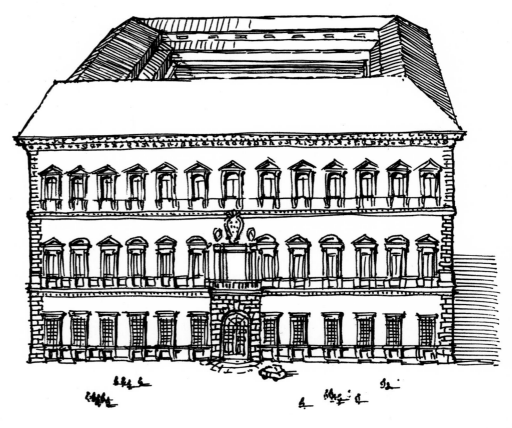

13. Campo dei Fiori

The piazzas of Rome are like outdoor rooms. Each has its own function and personality. The one in front of Palazzo Farnese acts as a formal reception room. The Campo dei Fiori, just a block away, is more like a family room. Every morning except Sunday, it houses a busy fruit and vegetable market. In the afternoons and evenings, when the stalls have been removed, it becomes a popular gathering place, with all its outdoor cafés and restaurants.

Streets of Rome

The streets of Rome are covered with a layer of cobblestones packed tightly on a bed of sand. Whenever work has to be done on underground pipes and cables, the cobbles are simply pried up. When the job is finished, they are fitted back together and pounded down.

The layout of many of the streets in the heart of the old city is quite random. For centuries people built into or on top of ancient ruins or wherever they could find space. The resulting maze would have given the engineers of the empire a serious case of the heebius-jeebius. What it gives us is continually changing views of the sky.

15. Torre Millina

The political instability of the Middle Ages provoked powerful families to build tall, crenelated towers right next to their homes. These structures offered a good view of the neighborhood as well as a convenient place to hide if their owners didn't like what they saw.

14. Santa Maria della Pace

Although the church was originally built in the fifteenth century, the baroque façade was redesigned in the seventeenth. While some parts of it recede, others project out to meet us. This is a stone wall with so much life it almost seems to be breathing. The small piazza in front of the church was enlarged when the façade was built so that carriages could turn around more easily.

16. Sant'Agnese in Agone

This church, begun in 1652, was built over the ruins of a much earlier church dedicated to Saint Agnes. As in most Christian churches of this period, a large dome covers the intersection of the two main axes. The little building that sits on top of the dome is called a lantern, perhaps because its windows help to light the space below.

17. Piazza Navona

Sant'Agnese is just one of the buildings overlooking Piazza Navona. This space is long and narrow because it exactly follows the shape of a first-century racetrack. The mostly seventeenth-century buildings enclosing the piazza today were built on the remains of the stone seats that originally surrounded the track. The fountain in the center of the piazza was designed by a sculptor named Bernini. It represents the four major rivers of the world and supports an Egyptian obelisk.

18. Sant'Ivo alla Sapienza

This church, dating from the middle of the seventeenth century, is actually part of a palazzo that once housed the University of Rome. Unless the front door of the palazzo is open, you can only see the dome and the lantern. But the spiral cap atop the lantern, ringed by stone torches, is an unforgettable landmark. It was designed by an architect named Borromini, and where he got the idea, who knows? Maybe from a fancy dessert.

19. Pantheon

If you think Sant'Ivo's cap is a little wacky, how about a building with a permanent hole in the roof? The Pantheon was designed by the Emperor Hadrian in the second century as a temple to all the gods. It replaced an earlier temple built by Marcus Agrippa, whose name appears below the pediment and above the huge Egyptian granite columns of the portico. The interior space is enclosed by a round drum on top of which sits a huge concrete dome. Trapezoidal recesses called coffers were built into the dome to reduce its weight. The only source of light is that hole in the roof, called an oculus. Not only the sun enters there, but also rain, snow, and whatever else happens to be falling from the sky.

The building is in excellent shape, because in the sixth century it was reconsecrated (like the Temple of Hercules) as a Christian church.

20. Piazza di Sant'Ignazio

In front of the imposing façade of the church of Sant'Ignazio di Loyola is a symmetrical piazza surrounded by buildings linked by curvilinear shapes. It was created a hundred years after the church was begun, in a style called rococo. If you thought the baroque façade of Santa Maria della Pace was exuberant, one spin around this space will leave you giddy.

21. The Gesù

The Church of the Jesuits was built between 1568 and 1584. It was begun by the architect Vignola and finished after his death by della Porta, who designed the façade. It contains a wide central space called a nave, along both sides of which are a number of smaller chapels. Those wide scroll buttresses that so inspired our pigeon were designed to gracefully link the height of the nave with that of the lower side chapels.

22. House of Lorenzo Manilo

Lorenzo Manilo built this house in the mid-fifteenth century. Swept up in the revival of interest in Rome's ancient past, he had a variety of building fragments, some quite large, inserted into the wall during construction. With the accumulation over the centuries of wires and pipes, altered windows and neon signs, this wall has become something of a gallery of Roman history as well as a tribute to the importance and effect of continual recycling.

SPQR

These letters stand for the Latin phrase
Senatus Populusque Romanus,
which means
"the Senate and the people of Rome."
You can find the entire phrase
carved in stone
above the Forum's triumphal arches.
The letters, which are cast
onto manhole covers and fountains and
emblazoned on the sides of city buses and taxis,
link modern Rome with its rich past and contribute
to an ongoing and reassuring sense of continuity.

Thank you Ruthie, Walter, Donna, Ezio, Laura, Tom, Susan
David, Lois, Alex, Colin, Liz, and Charlotte
for patience, advice, criticism, and encouragement,
or any combination thereof.

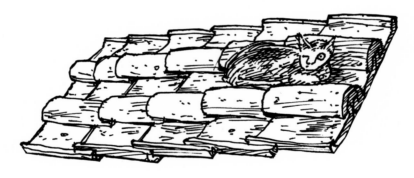

Walter Lorraine *wr* Books

Copyright © 1997 by David Macaulay
Library of Congress Cataloging-in-Publication Data
Macaulay, David.
Rome antics / David Macaulay.
p.   cm.
Summary: A pigeon carrying an important message takes the reader
on a unique tour which includes both ancient and modern parts of the
city of Rome.
ISBN 0-395-82289-3
[1. Rome — Fiction.   2. Homing pigeons — Fiction.]   I. Title.
PZ7.M1197Ro   1997
[Fic — dc21   CIP 97-20941
Printed in the United States of America
HOR 10 9 8 7 6 5 4 3 2 1